Stories from

Welsh History

told for children by Elisabeth Sheppard-Jones

JOHN JONES

STORIES FROM WELSH HISTORY

First edition May 1990
Revised edition 1995
Re-publication with new cover designed by Chris Neale, March 1998

Illustrations by John Shackell

ISBN 1 871083 70 2

Printed by John Penri Press, Saint Helen's Road, Swansea

Published by
JOHN JONES PUBLISHING LTD
Clwydfro Business Centre
Ruthin
North Wales
LL15 1NJ

Contents

Illustrations

The Dream of Macsen Wledig

In the days towards the end of the Roman occupation of Britain, there lived a Roman called Maximus. The Welsh called him Macsen Wledig (Wledig meaning in Welsh lord or noble), and said he was a wise and handsome man who ruled from Rome. They told a story about him that became a legend. It seemed that, when on a hunting expedition from Rome, Macsen rested in the heat of the midday sun and, under a shady tree, he fell asleep. He had a curious dream and this is what he dreamed.

He was moving slowly along a deep valley when he came to a mountain as high as heaven itself. He climbed the mountain with more ease than he had expected and, when he reached the top, there in front of him, stretching as far as the eye could see, was a land of great beauty. He climbed down the mountain and reached a wide river over which he swam and then followed its course until he came to the mouth of the river where it reached the sea. There was a great city built there and in the city Macsen could see a great castle. And also at the mouth of the river was a fleet of ships. One of these ships was bigger than the rest and had planks not of wood but of gold and silver and the bridge of the ship was of pure ivory. Macsen climbed aboard and away sailed this beautiful ship over the sea until it came to an island and here again was the mouth of another river and beyond it is a range of mountains and a stretch of woodland. Macsen disembarked from the ship and there, in front of him, he saw another castle, even more magnificent than the one he had seen before.

As the gate of the castle was open, Macsen walked through it and into the great hall where the roof was of gold and the walls encrusted with jewels. There were couches and chairs around the hall and these were of gold and, in front of them, were tables of silver. At one of these tables two red-haired young men were playing a game of gwyddbwyll which was a Welsh board game, something like chess. These lads were both dressed in black brocade and their bright hair was held in place by crowns in which sparkled diamonds, rubies and emeralds. Beyond them was seated an old man in a chair of ivory and

The Dream of Macsen Wledig

on his arms were gold bangles and on his fingers, gold rings. He was carving figures for the game of gwyddbwyll and did not look up when Macsen moved towards him. Bemused by the splendour of this place, it was a short time before Macsen's eyes settled on the far end of the hall and there, facing him, was a maiden of such beauty that she was as dazzling as the brightest sun. She was wearing a robe of pure silk and a cloak embroidered with jewels and pearls. She rose to meet Macsen, almost as if she was expecting him. He threw his arms round her and rested his cheek against hers. As he was about to kiss this lady whom he now loved with all his heart, his hunting dogs, who had been lying at his side beneath the tree under which he slept, began to bark, ready again for the chase, and their barking, together with the clang of the spears of his huntsmen, awoke Macsen from his dream.

For many days and many nights Macsen could think of nothing but the maiden of his dreams. He neglected his work and his play, his friends and his servants. One of his best friends decided he must speak to this sad ruler of Rome.

'What ails you, Macsen Wledig?' he asked.

'I am sad because of my dreams. I am happy only when I am asleep and can see my love again. Perhaps it is best that you send for the wise men of Rome for I badly need their help.'

This was done and Macsen told them of his dream and of the maiden whom he loved.

'Lord, this is what we advise,' said the leader of the wise men. 'Send out messengers to all parts of the earth until they find the land of which you dream and the castle in which lives this maiden of whom you speak.'

Macsen did as was suggested. For one year, his messengers scoured the lands far and wide. Finally, they came to the mouth of the first river about which Macsen had dreamt and to the second where was the island. Then they found the castle of Macsen's dreams and the two young men playing their game and the old man carving the figures and they saw a lovely maiden whose name they discovered was Elen. In fact, they had travelled through Italy and across France, over the island of Britain, across Britain to the west which was Wales and found the castle of Caernarfon.

'Behold!' cried the messengers, 'we have found that which our master saw in his dream.'

Then they explained to Elen the reason for their coming and said that Macsen's great wish was to marry her.

'If indeed he loves me,' Elen's reply, 'let him come and tell me this himself.'

By day and night the messengers travelled back to Rome where they gave their master the news of their success.

Immediately Macsen set out with them over the sea and the land. When he came to Wales he instantly recognised the fair country he had seen only in his dreams. There was the castle and the young men and the old man and, above all, looking radiant, was the lovely Elen. He threw his arms around her and, that night, they were married.

Macsen, on his journey, had conquered Britain and Elen asked as her wedding dowry that the land might be given for her father to rule over, and Macsen built two more castles for his bride, one at Caerleon and one at Carmarthen. For seven years Macsen and Elen lived in Wales but, on the eighth, they went back to Rome where a usurper had taken Macsen's place. With the help of his wife's brothers, two red-haired young men, Macsen regained Rome.

Later, when Macsen had unhappily been killed in battle for France, Elen returned to Caernarfon where she gathered around her many strong men of arms to protect Wales from attack by the Irish in the west and the Scots in the north. Elen became famous by her exploits and many a road or 'sarn' was afterwards called Sarn Elen in her memory.

Some of this story is legend; a little of it is fact. It is hard to tell which is which. It is certain the Maximus or Macsen existed as one of the last rulers of Roman Britain, and it is probable that he married Elen and that they lived together for many happy years.

The Feud

Fulke Fitzwarren was only seven years old when his father decided to send him to one Joce de Dinan of Ludlow Castle. The young boy cried, sulked and begged to be allowed to stay at home but it was the custom of the day to send boys to a household where they might learn to be knights and trained to be good soldiers. In the days of the Middle Ages there was much fighting and quarrelling among the many noble families who lived on the border of Wales, and Fulke's instructor Joce de Dinan had had a long feud with a family called de Lacy.

For many a long year, Fulke stayed at Ludlow, returning to his family for short periods every now and again. There had been for some years an uneasy peace between Joce and the de Lacys but matters changed abruptly when Fulke had just celebrated his seventeenth birthday. Early one summer morning Joce and Fulke had climbed to a high tower in the castle, as they did daily, to look out for any trouble there might be in the lands around.

'Quiet as usual, Fulke,' said Joce, as they mounted the stairs together.

'Indeed I hope so, my lord,' replied Fulke as they reached the battlements.

The lord and the boy looked towards the south where stretched peaceful green fields in which grazed cattle and sheep. But then they heard a great noise in the distance. Quickly the couple looked towards the north where it was far from peaceful. Approaching the castle was a large army, banners flying and armour glinting in the sun.

The alarm was quickly sounded and the castle instantly became a hive of activity.

'Go below and stay with the ladies,' Joce ordered Fulke.

The boy began to argue but Joce insisted that he was too young to join in the fighting.

At the head of 500 knights, men at arms and local townsfolk (or town burghers as they were called) Joce marched out to meet the de Lacys, for it was his old enemy who now attacked him.

The battle went well for Joce and many prisoners were taken.

The Feud

It was Walter de Lacy who had led the enemy forces and it was he Joce most wanted to capture. In the confusion this de Lacy had been cut off from his men and Joce saw him turn round and ride off on his horse. Joce mounted his own horse, and alone, began to chase after de Lacy. He caught him while still in sight of the castle and dragged him to the ground. De Lacy was about to submit when three of his knights appeared suddenly and, in defence of their lord, set upon the unfortunate Joce de Dinan.

Now Joce had two lovely daughters, Sybil who was dark as a raven and Hawyse who was as fair as a swan. Leaving Fulke in their quarters, the girls had gone to the castle battlements to watch the battle raging below. They saw to their horror what was happening to their father and their shrieks of alarm brought Fulke hurrying to the scene.

'What is the matter, Sybil? What ails you, Hawyse? I understand the battle is going well for us.'

'Alas, alas!' cried Sybil, 'our father is at this very moment being attacked by three of de Lacy's knights and there is no-one near to help him.'

'And where were you, brave Fulke, when you were needed,' asked Hawyse in an accusing voice.

'In your quarters where your father ordered me to be,' said Fulke.

'You are nothing but a wretched coward,' said Sybil, 'hiding like a baby in the ladies' quarters.'

'It was not my fault; I did as I was told,' Fulke defended himself.

'A man with more courage in his heart would have disobeyed such an order,' said the fair Hawyse.

'I'll show you that I am a brave and noble knight,' shouted Fulke, unable any longer to bear the reproaches of the two maidens. And he rushed down the stairs into the great hall, clapped on his head a rusty helmet that was lying there and seized an axe which was the only weapon to hand. He then rushed to the stables and mounted an old worn-out nag, and arrived just in time as Joce was being overwhelmed by Walter dy Lacy's men. Fulke smote the first knight, felling him to the ground; then the second knight he cut in two with his axe. The third knight he hit on his helmet of white steel until it split in half. This last man was a near relation of Walter de Lacy, by the name of Arnold and, although Fulke had wounded him, he was not killed. He and Walter de Lacy were taken to the castle by some of Joce's men who had now arrived on the scene.

Sir Joce turned to Fulke who, with the visor of his helmet down, was not recognisable.

'Friend burgher,' said Joce, 'you are strong and brave and, without your help, I should now be a dead man. I am grateful to you and from this day on you may live with me and I shall be your protector.'

'Sire, do you not recognise me?' asked Fulke and removed the rusty helmet. 'I am Fulke Fitzwarren for whom you have cared during many a year.'

Joce was astonished. 'My son, it was a good move I made when I consented to take you as a pupil. You have amply rewarded me.'

The two important prisoners, Walter de Lacy and his kinsman Arnold, were treated with courtesy and kindness. Arnold was a particularly handsome man and it was not long before Sybil was charmed by his attentions to her. Indeed, she agreed to marry him.

'But I can only do so when you are a free man and welcomed as such by my father,' she told him.

'Help me and my cousin Walter to escape then,' implored Arnold.

After some persuasion, Sybil agreed to help him. She used the familiar method of knotting sheets together and the two nobles climbed out of her bedroom window and departed from the castle.

The next morning Joce arose early and, seeing that all was well as he surveyed the countryside, he descended into his apartments to wash himself and to eat his breakfast. He called for his prisoner, Sir Walter, to join him for so high did Sir Joce regard Sir Walter, he would never wash nor eat without him. His knights and servants searched the castle and the vast grounds but nowhere could the prisoner be found. Un-expectedly, Sir Joce did not worry much about this but his generosity was not returned and there continued to be skirmishes between Sir Joce and Sir Walter.

There was peace for a while and this was when Fulke married Joce's daughter Hawyse. He had always been fond of both daughters but it was Hawyse whom he loved. She had apologised to him for her accusation about his cowardice and he had kissed her pale cheek and professed his love.

'We shall be married here at Ludlow which is more home to me than anywhere else in the world,' he promised her, 'and the Bishop of Hereford shall perform the ceremony.'

There followed many days and nights of merrymaking and celebration, after which the whole family party left for a visit elsewhere. Thirty knights and seventy soldiers only were left to guard the castle against possible attack by the de Lacys. Sybil, too, had decided to remain in Ludlow, in spite of the entreaties from her sister and brother-in-law that she should go with them on their prolonged honeymoon. Sybil stayed behind for a good reason. She wanted to see the man she loved, Sir Arnold Lacy and, when the others had departed, she sent word to him, telling him that the window through which he and Sir Walter had escaped would be open and that he might visit her at any time.

Arnold apparently did not love Sybil as much as she loved him. He realised that a visit to her might offer an opportunity for him to conquer the castle while Joce de Dinan was absent. Sybil had sent her lover a silk cord that she usually fastened round the waist of her gown. It was the exact measurement from her window to the ground. Arnold chose a cloudy, moonless night to keep his assignation. He brought with him a light leather ladder but, more important, he also brought with him a thousand armed men whom he bade to remain hidden until he told them otherwise.

'Sybil,' he called softly, 'Sybil my beloved, I have come to you. My ladder is the exact length of the silk cord you sent me.'

Sybil appeared at the window, her heart beating at the sight of the man she loved. At his bidding, she fixed the top of the ladder firmly against the sill of the window and Arnold climbed up it and into her arms.

While Sybil and Arnold talked of love, the ladder remained where it was against the wall. As daybreak approached, a hundred of de Lacy's men stealthily climbed the ladder. A sentinel was hurled from the watch tower and those knights and soldiers who had been left behind were slaughtered in their beds. Then the gates of the castle were opened and the rest of the de Lacy men poured in – and the castle was theirs.

Meanwhile, poor Sybil, aghast at what had happened and stricken by Arnold's treachery, seized his sword and plunged it into Arnold's heart. He died at once and Sybil clung to his dead body, rocking herself to and fro in her sorrow.

'Oh, Arnold, how I loved you,' she sighed, 'how could you have behaved so badly to me? Through my foolish love for you, my family has been betrayed and I wish to live no longer.'

With these words, she arose and moved to the window. The courtyard below was full of jostling soldiers. Sybil gave one last sigh, took a last look at the man she had loved so much, and threw herself out of the window.

Of course, later Fulke Fitzwarren and Joce de Dinan had their revenge on the de Lacys for the death of Sybil and the men who died in the castle but nothing was ever solved and the terrible feud between them continued to cause further deaths and unhappiness.

The Mother of Wales

Catherine de Beraine was descended from Henry VII, her grandfather being the king's illegitimate son. Henry had made him Constable of Beaumaris and given him large sums of money. When he married the heiress of a family called Penrhin, he became very wealthy as his bride brought him a good dowry. He had only one child, a daughter who, as a wealthy kinswoman and later an orphan, was made a ward by Queen Elizabeth I. Elizabeth was young at the time and her ward, being very pretty and popular, proved too much competition to the vain queen, so she was not kept long at court. Instead, she was offered as a bride to the nobility of Wales. Maurice of Beraine won the prize and from this marriage, too, there was one child, another girl. Her name was Catherine and she was even richer than her ancestors and clever, lively and good-looking into the bargain. She married a Salusbury of Llewenny, another wealthy man, but he died young and his youthful wife went sorrow-fully (or so it seemed) to his funeral.

Salusbury had had two close friends, Sir Richard Clough and Maurice Wynne of Gwydir, and both of these men were in love with Catherine. On the way to the church for the funeral services, Richard comforted the sorrowing widow.

'You will always have me to lean upon, my dear lady,' he told her.

'You are kind, Sir Richard,' replied the lady. 'I am but a frail woman and do not know how I shall manage now my husband has gone. Life is very hard.'

She wiped away her tears and put a fine linen handkerchief to her eyes. Sir Richard patted her on the shoulder.

'I have long loved you, Catherine,' he said, 'and now that you are alone, I should be glad if you will do me the honour of becoming my wife.'

This was not perhaps a very tactful moment for a proposal and one would have expected Catherine to reject his advances but Sir Richard was also a wealthy man and, rich though Catherine was herself, she was not averse to a further fortune.

'Maybe it is not right to accept such an offer when we are

on the way to my husband's funeral but, nevertheless, though you take me by surprise, I do accept you.'

She had accepted Sir Richard before they had even reached the church. The service over, Maurice Wynne approached the widow to offer his condolences. Taking her hand, he said to her quietly, 'This may not be the right moment but I have to declare my love for you, Catherine. Could you ever find it in your heart to become my wife?'

Catherine managed to hide a smile and dabbed once again at her eyes.

'You do me honour, Maurice Wynne,' she said, 'but I regret to say you are a little late. I have already agreed to marry Sir Richard Clough.'

Poor Maurice was amazed and shocked. He thought he had been a little premature with his offer but it had never occurred to him that he might have been forestalled. He managed to pull himself together and, taking both her hands in his, he said, 'I cannot pretend that your news has not come as a surprise and I am saddened to hear you are to marry someone else. Nevertheless, may I ask one favour of you?'

'Certainly,' replied Catherine, 'although I cannot promise, of course, to grant you what you wish.'

'Heaven knows I do not want any harm to come to Sir Richard, my rival though he is, but if by some misfortune you are widowed again, will you reconsider my offer of marriage?'

Here was yet another rich man; Catherine felt herself to be doubly blessed. She was too overcome to speak but she nodded her head and squeezed Maurice Wynne's hands.

When he was only forty years old, Sir Richard died and Maurice Wynne could scarcely believe his luck. He and Catherine were married a month or so after the funeral of her second husband. However, Maurice did not live long to enjoy his newly wedded bliss and died a few years later. Had Catherine not been highly regarded in the Vale of Clwyd where she lived, it might have seemed that she was disposing of husbands rather too quickly. No sooner was Maurice cold in his grave when she had another proposal from yet another rich man, Edward Thelwell of Plas-y-Ward. Thus Catherine had married into four of the most powerful families in North Wales-

Salusbury, Clough, Wynne and Thelwell. Her descendents from these four husbands were as the sands of the sea and thus it was that she was given the name of Mam Cymru or the Mother of Wales.

Catherine Clough's husband, the most famous of the four, did give her a little trouble. He had built for them a house near Denbigh called Bachygraig. At the top of this house was a windowless room and, in this, Richard would shut himself at night, forbidding anyone to enter while he was there. The country people believed he had conversations with the Devil. Catherine apparently had similar suspicions. The legend grew up that, on one occasion, she crept quietly up the stairs and looked through the keyhole. To her amazement, she saw her husband and the Devil chatting together. In horror, she opened the door and confronted them.

'My dear husband,' she cried, 'what are you doing in such evil company?'

'My dear wife, please do not interfere. This gentleman and I are having a serious philosophical discussion. It is of no interest to you.'

Catherine moved towards him as if to protect him from the dark stranger. The Devil glowered at her, his eyes flashing fire, and she was rooted to the spot. Then the Devil seized hold of Sir Richard and dashed right through the wall with him. Sir Richard was found, shivering in the garden, and refused to discuss the matter with his wife. After this, Catherine's life with her other husbands, Wynne of Gwydir and Edward Thelwell of Plas-y-Ward must have been comparatively peaceful!

Ellen Gethin

There lived once, in a valley in Radnorshire, a well-known family called Vaughan. One of the tales told about these Vaughan concerned one who lived just before the Wars of the Roses. Her name was Ellen Gethin or Ellen the Terrible. This makes her sound an unattractive character but she was called Terrible only because of one single act and not because her behaviour was always savage.

The home of Ellen Vaughan and her brother David was called Hergest Court and their cousins Vaughan lived at Tretower in Breconshire. As so often in Welsh history, the Vaughans had family quarrels as to which branch should be head of the clan. Now Ellen was particularly devoted to her brother and was alarmed when one day he told he was to have a meeting with Tir Sion (or Long John), a Vaughan from Tretower.

'I beg you not to go, David,' said his sister. 'Tir Sion is a dangerous man and you know how bitterly he feels towards us. Stay at home and forget about him.'

'My honour is at stake,' replied David, 'Tir Sion has asked to meet me and it would be cowardly to refuse.'

'Well then, go in peace; do not provoke our cousin but discuss family matters calmly and with dignity.'

This David promised to do and would have kept his promise had Tir Sion not been in an angry, fighting mood.

Ellen awaited her brother's return with some anxiety. He had departed early in the morning for a meeting place on the borders of Radnorshire and Breconshire. The morning passed and so did the afternoon. Ellen paced up and down the terrace of Hergest Court. The sun set, throwing long shadows across the garden, and still David had not returned. As Ellen was about to leave the terrace and go into the house, she saw two of the Vaughan servants approaching the house from the garden. They were carrying the body of a young man. Ellen put her hand to her mouth to stifle a scream and ran swiftly to the spot where her dead brother had now been laid.

'What happened, what happened?' cried Ellen, getting down

Ellen Gethin

on her knees and hugging to her breast her beloved brother's curly head.

'Tir Sion Vaughan, my lady,' said one of the servants, 'lost his temper when the master suggested Vaughans of Hergest should be the head of the family. He drew his sword and pierced the heart of your brother. He did not have a chance but died instantly with no time to defend himself.'

Ellen was too grief-stricken to cry or to speak but, there and then, she vowed to have vengeance on her cousin. She did so in a dramatic fashion.

The following week there was to be a great archery competition held in the neighbourhood of the Tretower Vaughans. Ellen spent her time practising at the archery butts. She had always been a proficient archer but she needed to be perfect. Tir Sion was known to be a particularly skilful archer.

When the day of the competition arrived, Ellen dressed herself in some of her brother's clothes and tucked her hair into one of his caps. With her slim figure and thus disguised, she looked like a very handsome youth. She needed this disguise because only males could enter the competition. It was not thought right that women should be archers. Ellen slipped off across country to the gathering and arrived just in time to see her cousin fire his last and, as it proved, victorious shot.

'Well done,' she called, striding forward from the admiring crowd. 'You shoot very well, my lord.'

'Better than any other in Wales,' boasted Tir Sion.

'I doubt that,' said Ellen.

Tir Sion frowned. 'You are an insolent boy,' he said.

'Not insolent but honest, sire. I know of one who shoots better than you.'

'Why did he not appear for the competition then?' growled Tir Sion.

'Because he was too late but he is here now.' Ellen smiled at her cousin, hiding her true feelings.

Tir Sion looked about him. The crowd began to murmur.

'Bring him forth,' bellowed Tir Sion, 'and we shall see who is the better man.'

'He is here,' said Ellen quietly, 'at your side. I am he.'

Tir Sion looked astonished, 'You a mere lad and think you can beat me? All right, let us see you in action then.'

'As you will, my lord,' said Ellen, fixing an arrow to her bow. Carefully she drew back the bow, released the bowstring and let the arrow fly to the target. It hit near the gold, the centre of the target.

'A good shot', admittted Tir Sion, 'but possible to beat.'

His arrow flew through the air and landed very near Ellen's arrow.

Tir Sion ran across the grass and up to the target that he might judge whose arrow was nearer to the gold.

'Nothing much in it,' he called, 'but it would seem that I am a little nearer the gold than you.'

Ellen fixed another arrow to her bow and called back, 'Maybe that is true but this arrow will not miss its target; it is for you and not for the gold.'

Tir Sion was hit in the chest and collapsed to the ground. He was dead.

'So, I have my revenge,' murmured Ellen to herself, and she ran into the astonished crowd and was lost to view. Changing into her woman's clothes and releasing her long hair from the cap, she easily escaped from the scene of her crime. No-one ever discovered who was the stranger who shot Tir Sion.

This story has a happier end. Some years passed before Ellen met Tir Sion's brother and fell in love with him. The quarrel between the Vaughans of Hergest and the Vaughans of Tretower was satisfactorily resolved. Ellen married Lord Tretower and, later the bards sang her praises in stirring verse which may be read today. We are not told if Ellen ever revealed to her husband the truth about his brother's death.

The Wreck of the Spanish Galleon

Many ships have been wrecked off the coast of Wales and one particular hazard is a place, on the Gower Coast, called Worm's Head, a promontory which stretches out to sea. This rocky, dangerous spot has always struck terror into the hearts of seamen and is in strong contrast to the peaceful sandy bay of Rhosilli which lies off it.

In 1625 a Spanish galleon, loaded with gold, struck the rocks and drifted on to the deep sands of Rhosilli. It was a wild night, the waves crashing on the shore and the wind howling like a banshee but, remarkably, the crew all managed to get off the ship without harm or loss of life. The captain suggested to his men that they take as much gold as they could carry and leave the scene quietly without rousing suspicion. The dark stormy night made it difficult for the men to load themselves with many sovereigns but they stuffed what they could into their pockets. Then they slipped away into the night.

The next day, the captain was drinking at an inn when he met a man called Thomas.

'Judging from your accent,' said Thomas, 'I would guess you are a stranger in this country.'

The Spaniard nodded and, without more ado, boldly asked, 'Are you interested in buying a wreck?'

Thomas was very interested. 'Where is it?' he asked.

'Rhosilli Bay and safely beached on the sand.'

'And how much are you asking?'

'Not much to a gentleman like yourself,' replied the Spaniard. 'Name a figure.'

For an hour or so they argued over the price but finally Thomas handed over a bag of sovereigns and the wreck was his. The captain forgot to tell Thomas what the ship had been carrying and Thomas, having had a few drinks, forgot to ask. Indeed, for a time, he forgot he owned a wreck and, by the time he remembered, the ship had sunk too deep into the sand for him to be able to break it up.

Every now and again, as the years went by, someone on the beach would come across a gold piece and thus word got around

The Wreck of the Spanish Galleon

that the wreck was a treasure ship and Talbot, Lord of the Manor, put in a claim for it. Nothing further happened until fifty years later when Mansell, another Lord of a Manor who had no actual rights to it, came to Rhosilli one night and got away with a hoard of gold. Fearing the Talbot's wrath, he went abroad where he died, apparently, a rich but unhappy man, made guilty by his crime. It was said his ghost returned to the scene where it drove up and down the shore in a black coach with four grey horses. A descendent of the ghostly Mansell had better fortune as the result of a wreck. Mansell of Margam was the local Lord of the Manor and, in 1787, a vessel carrying orange trees was wrecked on the nearby coast. The trees were apparently a gift for the King of England from the King of Portugal and this cargo was claimed by Mansell as his manorial right. The orangery, which can be seen to this day at Margam Abbey, is said to be the largest in the world.

Early in the nineteenth century, the Rhosilli wreck, which had been invisible under the sand for a long time, suddenly re-appeared on the occasion of a particularly low tide. This time the crew of a smuggling boat landed on the beach and took a fortune from the wrecked galleon. They were seen doing this by a couple of local people and soon the news spread around and hoards of people descended on the Bay. Not only the locals appeared but strangers, too, from some distance away. Eager and greedy for gold, the two factions started fighting on the beach. Talbot, as true Lord of the Manor, soon put a stop to the rioting and decided that he himself would examine the wreck, and a proper search was made. Still more dowlone were discovered before the wreck again disappeared, only to re-appear the following year to reveal more gold than ever. It was then that a descendent of the original Thomas arrived on the scene and faced Mr. Talbot.

'I have more right to this wreck than you,' this Thomas said, 'and the gold should be mine.'

'How is your claim better than mine?' asked the Lord of the Manor.

'In that my ancestor bought the wreck off a Spanish captain two hundred years ago.'

'A long time ago and much has happened since then, and

I would remind you that I am Lord of the Manor and therefore have rights to any ship wrecked on my coast.'

A bitter argument followed until, finally, an angry Mr. Talbot said, 'Enough of this; the wreck has caused me nothing but trouble. You shall not have it and I will not have it. Here and now, I give all rights to the people of Rhosilli. And that shall be the end of the matter.'

So it was that after that time, the local people continued to take little hauls of coins until the treasure finally came to an end.

Saint Melangell

Brochwel, Prince of Powys during the 8th century, was fond of hunting, especially in the lovely country around Llangynog in North Wales. On one occasion, he and his men were enjoying a day's sport when they saw a particularly fine hare racing across a field in front of them.

'Follow the hare!' cried Brochwel as one of his huntsmen blew the hunting horn. The great array of men, horses and dogs immediately began to move in the direction of the animal. The hare's speed increased and so did the speed of the huntsmen. Temporarily the quarry was lost as the hare darted into a copse but it was not long before the dogs picked up its scent but, once among the trees, the dogs suddenly came to an adrupt halt. They began to whine and howl but refused to move.

'Urge on those dogs,' ordered Brochwel but, although the huntsmen cracked their whips and called to them, the dogs still refused to move.

'Well, we'll go on without them,' shouted Brochwel, angry with the obstinate dogs but puzzled also at their strange behaviour. He and his men and horses pushed on until they came to a clearing in the wood where, kneeling at prayer, was a beautiful maiden and, peeping out from under the hem of her dress, was the hare they had been hunting.

'There it is, sire,' cried one of the huntsmen. 'There's the hare!'

'Go and get it then,' said Brochwel. 'It will make a very fine supper dish, to be sure.'

The dogs had moved even further away and now the horses were neighing and shivering with fright. The young girl finished her prayer and rose to her feet, still guarding the hare.

'Do not touch this hare; he is under my protection,' she said coldly, looking Brochwel straight in the eye and showing no fear.

At a nod from Brochwel, one of the huntsmen lifted his horn and was about to blow it, when he found the instrument had stuck to his lips. Some of the other huntsmen began to laugh but Brochwel gazed at the maiden in astonishment.

'Have you put a spell on us, my lady, just to save the life of one small hare?' he asked.

Saint Melangell

She said nothing but only inclined her head.

'It is a miracle,' announced Brochwel. 'And what, fair lady, do they call you?'

'My name is Melangell and I am an Irish princess,' came the reply.

Brochwel addressed his huntsmen. 'The hunt is off,' he said, 'no-one shall hunt the hare.' Then he asked Melangell what she was doing in Wales to which she replied, 'A marriage was arranged for me to a man of ill-repute and bad honour. I came here to escape from him and have lived here in the copse for fifteen years; you are the first human I have seen in all that time.'

'And have you not been lonely and unhappy?' Brochwel spoke gently to her.

'No, I have had the animals and I have communed with God. It is a peaceful life. I have no regrets – well, perhaps just one . . .'

'And, pray, what is that?' asked Brochwel.

'I should dearly have loved to build a church to the glory of God but, alas, I have no lands nor wealth with which to do this.'

Brochwel was deeply moved by this devout lady and, after a few minutes' thought, he said, 'I own all the land hereabouts and it is in my power to give to you the land at Pennant and the money for both a church and a convent.'

And so it was that Pennant Melangell had its church and the maiden became Saint Melangell, the patron saint of hares. The hunt seldom chased hares in that part of the land, and the local people, if they saw one being hunted, would shout out, 'Saint Melangell protect you,' and, sure enough, the hare would always escape.

Owain Glyndwr and Lord Grey

Ruthin Castle had been built by Edward I and was later, in 1399, occupied by an Englishmen, Lord Grey, who ruled somewhat brutally over the surrounding land. He was a typical medieval baron, exacting dues and taxing traders and markets and generally making himself very unpopular with his Welsh subjects. He must also have been something of a fool and was probably the cause of the last uprising of the Welsh against the English which was led by Owain Glyndwr.

It so happened that Owain's property, which was a large one, bordered that of Lord Grey. Now Owain was a man of some importance and was the social equal of his neighbour; the Welsh possibly thought him superior as he was descended from the Prince of Powys. It is doubtful that, at this time, Owain was restless or looking for trouble but, as so often happened, he and Grey had a dispute about a boundary. During this argument, Grey seized part of Glyndwr's land and Owain decided to go to London to seek justice at the High Court.

'I wish redress from Lord Grey who has illegally seized some of my land,' Owain told the officials.

'And who, may I ask are you?' said one of the officials, 'and why should we listen to your complaint?'

'I am Owain Glyndwr,' came the answer, 'and of some importance in my own country.'

'And what country is that?' sneered the official.

'A country of great pride, a country of poets, of musicians and brave fighters. The country of Wales.'

'Oh that country!' The official sniggered. 'I am sorry but, in the circumstances, there is nothing we can do for you. We are not able to give you any sort of hearing. You yourself will have to settle your quarrel with Lord Grey.'

Owain, feeling himself snubbed by the English officials, decided to do exactly as they had suggested – settle his quarrel with Lord Grey in his own way.

On his return to Wales, he gathered his men about him and attacked the Castle of Ruthin, looting the town and burning much of it to the ground. Lord Grey was absent at the time but soon gathered his men about him and his army and that of Owain met at Bryn Saith Marchog. The Lord of Ruthin was defeated and captured. Captured with him was another English lord, Edmund Mortimer.

Lord Grey was one of King Henry IV's men and the King was angry at what had happened and sent an envoy to Owain, demanding news of the prisoner.

Owain greeted the envoy and treated him with the hospitality due to his rank.

'May I ask what brings you here,' said Owain. 'It surely is not to give me greetings from the King.' Owain remembered well the poor way he had been treated when in London.

'He does, in fact, send greetings,' replied the envoy diplomatically, 'but he would also like to know what has happened to Lord Grey.'

'He is imprisoned but well cared for, which is more than he deserves after his treachery to me.'

'To come to the point, my lord, King Henry wants him released as he is a loyal servant of the crown.'

Owain smiled and fingered his beard. 'Surely he does not expect me to release Lord Grey just because it suits him for me to do so.'

'He is prepared to pay a ransom,' said the envoy.

'Oh a ransom is it? And what, pray, does he think Lord Grey is worth?'

'A few thousand marks,' suggested the King's man.

'Let us be exact; let us say ten thousand marks,' snapped Owain.

'Ten thousand'. That's a fortune; I do not know that the King will agree to that amount.'

'Return to him then and say I will take no less.' Thus Owain ended the conversation.

So the envoy returned to London where the King, although appalled at the size of the ransom, finally agreed. Back the envoy travelled to Wales.

'I have brought the ten thousand marks you demanded,' he said.

'I have a further demand now,' said Owain.

The envoy turned pale. 'I do not think the King will grant anything else.'

'Then Lord Grey stays where he is and dies a prisoner.'

'I – I cannot make any promises,' stammered the envoy, 'but, perhaps if it is not too much . . .'

'I want the ownership of Lord Grey's manor in Kent,' demanded Owain.

Back to London went the weary messenger and once again received the King's consent to the demand. In Wales Owain received the news with delight. It had taken a year for the ransom to be settled and Lord Ruthin was set free. But, before the royal messenger had departed, Owain had something further to say to him.

'There has been no mention of any ransom to be paid for Lord Edmund Mortimer who is also my prisoner.'

The messenger smiled this time. 'King Henry will pay no ransom for that particular lord; you can keep him as long as you like.'

The truth was that, whereas Grey was a loyal subject of the King, Mortimer was not to be trusted for he himself had a claim to the throne. The King was quite happy to have such a dangerous rival permanently in Owain's clutches. As a result of this, Glyndwr made a faithful ally of his prisoner who was freed and married Catherine, one of Glyndwr's daughters and therefter fought by Owain's side.

The affair of Lord Grey and the King's contemptuous attitude to Glyndwr embittered the Welshman and it was then that although he was already middle-aged, he began to rouse his fellow Welshmen into rebellion against England. The Glyndwr rising was one of destructive ferocity and united many of those in both north and south Wales who had previously been at each others' throats. Now it was the whole of Wales against England. Owain's supporters called him the Prince of Wales, and for many years the fight continued unabated.

Owain was a great fighter. In his early days he had fought in both Ireland and France and also in a battle at Berwick on Tweed. His bard Iolo Goch, said that there he drove men before him with a broken spear and that the grass withered at his fiery attack. He was favoured at the beginning of his rebellion with such good luck that his followers regarded him as a magician who could even change the very weather when needed. Owain was himself a superstitious man who believed in his fortune as he read it in the stars. Owain had the support of France and of a few English nobles who were out of favour with King Henry but, by 1410, his luck deserted him and the Welsh were defeated. By now, Henry V was on the throne and twice offered Glyndwr a pardon but the old man, as he now was, refused to accept, preferring to remain a hunted outlaw.

No-one knew where or how Owain Glyndwr died. No bard sang of his death because no Welshman believed he had died. He became a national hero: one day he would again lead his people to victory. He then became a legend and, like the immortal King Arthur, it is said he lies somewhere in the Welsh mountains waiting the call to return whenever Wales should need him.

Rhys ap Thomas

Chief among the Welshmen who helped to put on the throne Henry Tudor was Rhys ap Thomas, a great lord of south west Wales and a man who had in his veins the blood of ancient Welsh princes. When Richard III was king, Rhys pretended allegiance to him.

'Your Majesty, the man you fear, Henry Tudor, Henry of Richmond, will advance only over my body,' assured Rhys.

The King accepted this assurance not guessing that, though Rhys would not lie to him, he was a cunning man.

Henry landed with his forces at Dale, a secluded bay near Milford Haven. It was a Sunday evening and Rhys ap Thomas was there to greet the man who was to become the first Welsh king of England. Henry saw Rhys approach, riding his famous horse, Llwyd y Bacse, and surrounded by his men. Rhys dismounted and Henry greeted him warmly, encouraged by the sight of so many Welshmen eager to help him.

'My lord,' said Rhys, 'I made a promise to King Richard.'

'A promise to that tyrant,' retorted Henry, wondering if this man was, in fact, an ally. 'What did you promise?'

'I swore that you would advance to London only over my body.'

Henry Tudor frowned. 'You mean you have no intention of helping me to victory?'

'No, that's not what I mean,' and to the astonishment of the crowd Rhys lay down on the ground.

'What are you doing, man?' Henry demanded to know. 'Get up at once.'

'Not until you have stepped over me,' grinned Rhys, and Henry and the company of men began to laugh. Henry moved towards Rhys's body and, with dignity, stepped over it. More laughter ensued before the plans for victory were discussed seriously.

Henry had already written to many Welsh lords, asking for their support and they did not let him down. 'Father Rhys,' as Henry was to call him, had seen to it that, for once, the Welsh princes would cease quarrelling among themselves. Some time before Henry's invasion, he had made famous his home, Carew Castle, by inviting to a great tournament the elite of Wales and,

Rhys ap Thomas

to everyone's surprise, they all accepted – Perotts, Wogans, Herberts, Morgans, Butlers, Vaughans and Mansells among them. Rhys was Governor of Wales and probably the wealthiest and greatest person in that country. The entertainment at Carew was lavish and lasted a week. And, due to Rhys's wisdom and influence, no sword was drawn in anger nor a cross word spoken. On the first day of the great festival, Rhys led his glittering throng, with drums beating and trumpets blowing, to hear mass from the Bishop of St. David's. His guests, brought together in peace for the first time, were among the many Welshmen who helped Henry Tudor to victory.

At the head of a considerable force, Rhys ap Thomas led his men through mid-Wales. 'A worthy sight it was to see,' went an old ballad, 'how the Welshmen rose wholly with Henry, and shogged them to Shrewsbury.'

From Shrewsbury, they marched on to Stafford and, finally to the battlefield of Bosworth where they joined with Henry's English supporters and Richard III was beaten and deposed. The new king had a Welshman's love of music and encouraged poets and bards. He took pains to stress his connection with Wales. His eldest son was christened Arthur, after the legendary king, and Henry employed heralds to trace his Welsh ancestry. He amply rewarded Rhys ap Thomas, making him virtual ruler of South Wales.

Lake Savaddan

Three men, Welsh lords, were returning from Brecon from the court of Henry II. It was winter and the journey had been hard but it was a fine day and, when they came to Lake Savaddan, surrounded by the green heights of the Brecon Beacons, they dismounted from their horses to rest a while . It was a still windless day, not a ripple on the lake and not a sound of any sort anywhere.

The three men were Milo, Earl of Hereford and Lord of Brecon; Payn Fitz John, Lord of Ewyas; and Griffith ap Rhys who was not lord of anywhere. Now Milo and Payn possessed rich districts but young Griffith possessed nothing very much although he came from a long and noble line.

There was a flock of wild fowl on the lake which caught Milo's attention.

'Seeing those birds over there,' he said to his companions, 'I am reminded of a Welsh tradition.'

'What tradition is that?' asked Payn.

'Well, it is said that the birds of Savaddan will only sing at the command of a natural prince of our country.'

Payn laughed. 'Griffith claims to be of nobler birth than either of us, let us now see which of the three of us is prince of our country.'

'That is a somewhat foolish suggestion,' said Milo, 'but nonetheless I'll go along with it, if Griffith agrees.'

Griffith had remained silent until now. 'I certainly agree,' he said. 'I have nothing to lose. Who shall go first?'

'Milo,' said Payn, 'as he is the eldest of us.'

'If the birds are going to sing, they'll certainly sing for me,' said Milo.

The three men moved to the edge of the lake; the sun shimmered on the water and shadows of the mountains shifted to and fro.

'Birds!' cried out Milo, his voice echoing across the lake. 'I, Milo, lord of Hereford and Brecon, command you to sing and acknowledge my noble birth.'

A few birds rose into the air, flapping their wings before

Lake Savaddan

returning to float serenely on the water. There was not a sound from them.

'Come on, birds, sing, sing!' shouted Milo impatiently. But no birds sang.

'You have failed, Milo' said Payn, 'it is obvious that the birds have no intention of obeying you. It is now my turn. Griffith is the youngest, so he can go last, if it should prove necessary which I doubt.'

Griffith smiled. 'You are wasting your time, Payn; I am the only true noble of the three of us.'

Milo and Payn laughed scornfully. 'You own nothing,' said Milo.

'It is nobility of birth which is at stake here,' said Griffith, 'not possession of lands. But, come along, Payn, issue your command if you will.'

Payn moved even nearer to the lake, his boots touching the edge of the water.

'Birds!' he cried out in a loud voice, 'I, Payn Fitz John, Lord of Ewyas, command you to sing and acknowledge my noble birth.'

Again, a few birds flapped their wings and a couple skimmed away into the distance. There was not a sound from them.

'Birds,' shouted Payn in an even louder voice. 'Sing, I command you to sing.' But no birds sang.

It was Griffith's turn to laugh. 'Both of you have failed,' he said, 'now we shall see if the birds will sing for me.'

'It's only a superstition,' muttered Milo, 'the birds will sing for no-one; after all, water birds make odd quacking noises; they do not really *sing* at all.'

'Let us mount our horses and continue our journey,' said Payn. 'Enough of this nonsense.'

'It is only fair that I should have my turn,' insisted Griffith and, after a short argument, Milo and Payn agreed.

To the astonishment of his friends, Griffith went down on his knees and began to pray as he would do on the eve of a battle. His prayer finished, he fixed his eyes on the flock of birds and, fairly quietly, he spoke to them.

'Birds,' he said, 'I, Griffith ap Rhys, a nobleman without possessions, command you to sing and acknowledge my noble birth.'

Milo and Payn were already mounting their horses when the birds all rose together, beating the water with their wings, and a chorus of the sweetest bird song filled the air.

'There, listen to that,' said Griffith triumphantly. 'Perhaps now you will acknowledge that I am indeed a prince of the land.'

Milo and Payn were too amazed at the sight and sound of the birds that they could only nod their heads. Griffith had won the day.

Gwilym Jones of Newland

Gwilym and his parents lived in the village of Newland near the town of Monmouth. He was a bright, lively boy and, when he was old enough to work, he asked his father if he might apply for a job in the town.

'They want a boy to help with the chores of the King's Head Inn,' he said. 'Do you think, father, that I might get the job?'

His father was delighted to know the boy might be working as they were a poor family and extra money was always welcome. He gladly encouraged the boy to apply for the job and this Gwilym did, and obtained the post.

Now some years later there came a young lady to help the innkeeper. She was a handsome woman, a cousin of the innkeeper, well-educated and full of charm. It was not long before Gwilym had fallen in love with her but she was a lady and he only a kitchen boy. However, as the girl was always sweet and pleasant to him, he decided he could lose nothing if he proposed to her. He was alone in the kitchen, peeling potatoes, when she came to ask if the meal was nearly ready.

'It won't be long, madam,' was the reply, 'and, while we are alone, I have something I should like to ask you.'

The lady was surprised at the serious manner of the scullion. She nodded her lovely head and Gwilym put down the knife he had been using and faced her.

'You are the most beautiful maiden I have ever seen and the sweetest; I should be honoured if you would consent to be my wife.' The words rushed out of his mouth almost before he had time to think. He was indeed a foolish lad if he thought this superior creature could ever agree to marry him. In fact, she began to laugh and her laughter hurt Gwilym more than a straight refusal would have done.

'Oh dear,' cried his lady love, 'you must be joking, Gwilym, indeed you must be joking. *Me* marry *you!* Why, I could have my pick of the finest gentlemen in Monmouth.' And, once again, she burst out laughing before hurrying from the kitchen.

Poor Gwilym was heartbroken. He realised he had been foolish but still he could not help loving this beautiful woman.

Gwilym Jones of Newland

He was in a hopeless situation and, unable to bear the sight of his loved one, he decided it would be better if he left the inn and never saw her again. But, before he went, knowing he might need to walk some distance before getting another job, he went to the shoemaker, a Mr. Joe King, to buy a pair of shoes. Saying he would pay for them later, he took the shoes and ran away from the inn and Monmouth.

There were many of the shoemaker's friends who accused Gwilym of being a rogue to leave the town without paying for his shoes but Joe King was not so upset.

'Gwilym Jones is a good lad; he'll pay me whenever he can,' he said.

The years went by, rolling one after the other. Whenever his name was mentioned, it was 'that wretched young man who ran away without paying Mr. King for his shoes.' Still the kindly shoemaker said, 'Gwilym is a good young man and will pay me when he can.'

After a while, even the shoes and Gwilym Jones were forgotten.

The young saplings planted by old Mr. and Mrs. Jones were now grown into trees in the garden of the little cottage at Newland. It was a fine spring morning and the daffodils and primroses were all in flower when an elderly man in a ragged coat, his back bent like a bow, crept through the village to the cottage where he sat down on the grass under the shadow of the trees. The woman who now lived in the cottage came out of the front door and saw the stranger in her garden.

'Good day to you, ma'am,' said Gwilym, for he it was. 'May I stay here a while and beg a drink of you from the well?'

'Certainly you may not,' snapped the woman. 'This is not a place for tramps and vagabonds. Go and get some water in another place.'

'I am tired,' said Gwilym. 'I have come a long way.'

'That's of no concern to me,' said the woman. 'Go along with you, get away from my cottage and my garden or I'll set the dog on you.' Behind her was a large dog, growling and showing his teeth. Gwilym quickly rose up and made his way to the nearest alehouse in Newland where he sat down on a bench outside. The innkeeper came out and asked him what he wished to order. Gwilym shook his head and, 'I'd like a glass of water,' he said, 'I have no money for beer.' The innkeeper frowned.

'Go away,' he said, 'off to the poorhouse with you. Do not sit here, taking up the room of a good customer.'

So off to the poorhouse went Gwilym, who had been away for thirty years. It seemed he had returned ragged and penniless and he tried to claim relief from the parish where his mother and father had lived all their lives.

'You have been too long away,' he was told, 'and, anyway, you left Newland once to work in Monmouth. There is nothing here for you.'

'I beg for your help,' pleaded Gwilym, 'all I want is a little food and drink and somewhere to lay my head. I'm an old man and I should like to end my days here and be buried in the grave where my parents lie.'

But no pity was shown him and he was sent, hungry and footsore, on his way to Monmouth. There, he was admitted into the poorhouse and made welcome. He lived there for a time and was loved and respected by all the paupers who surrounded him. He had not been there long when he made his way to the shoemaker who was living in the same small house next door to the King's Head Inn where Gwilym had worked when a young man.

'Do your remember me, Joe King?' asked Gwilym.

'No matter whether I do or not,' said Joe gazing at him with short-sighted eyes. 'You look as if you could do with a bite to eat,' and he took the old man into his kitchen and gave him some bread and cheese.

'Do you not remember me?' asked Gwilym again. 'A good for nothing scamp of a lad who worked at the King's Head and who cheated you out of a pair of shoes?'

'Well, well,' said old Joe King. 'I do remember a boy called Gwilym Jones – wild Will some folks called him – but he was no scamp and would pay me yet if he could. And surely I may forgive a poor fellow the value of a pair of shoes.'

Next morning the pauper was gone and there was a great fuss and much talk that he had gone off with the workhouse clothes. But a month later, a coach drew up to the workhouse and out of it got a fine, broad-shouldered gentleman, with a back as straight as a poplar tree. He carried a bundle under his arm, asked for the master of the poorhouse and handed over some old clothes. It was, long before the news spread around the town that poor old Will Jones had really been, all along, the Gwilym Jones of the city of London, who had a right to stand up to the King himself and was a rich man indeed. From the workhouse, Gwilym drove straight to the shoemaker and it was not easy to persuade Joe King that this great gentleman was the boy from Newland who ran away from the inn and made his fortune and owed him for a pair of shoes. After a long talk, Gwilym left a purse, heavy with gold sovereigns, on the shoemaker's table.

Gwilym had intended to do more for Newland than he did for Monmouth but, such had been his treatment in that village, he left in his will almshouses and money for the comfort of the poor people of Monmouth only. However, he was too good a man to bear malice so he also left the sum of five thousand pounds to the people of Newland, hoping to teach them that charity should always be given to those who appear to need it.

The French Invasion

It was a fine day at the end of February in the year 1797 when an English gentleman who was visiting Fishguard stopped to talk to a farmer who was busy cutting the hedgerows.

'A beautiful day, sir,' commented the farmer.

'Indeed it is,' replied the gentleman. 'I am a stranger in these parts and your Welsh sunshine has been very kind to me.'

They continued to chat about the weather and were exchanging news of the day when the Englishman's attention was suddenly taken by the sight of three frigates approaching Fishguard harbour below them.

'A fine sight there,' he said, 'three of our warships sailing towards us'.

From where the men were standing there was a good view of the sea. The farmer followed the gentleman's outstretched finger. He frowned, looked away over the fields for a moment, looked back and frowned again.

'Them's no British ships,' he said.

'But they are flying our colours,' was the reply.

'Them's not British ships,' repeated the farmer.

'But how would you, a farmer, know anything about ships?' asked the Englishman.

'I haven't always been a farmer. I went to sea when I was a young man and I can tell you from the look of those frigates, they are French. I'd stake my life on it.'

'French!' exclaimed the gentleman. 'But this is terrible. You should take a horse at once and muster the soldiers. I'll go down to the harbour and see what I can find out for I speak a little French, and perhaps, after all, there is nothing to fear.'

Without more ado, the farmer ran to his stables, saddled his fastest horse and rode towards Haverfordwest where the nearest soldiers were stationed.

Meanwhile the Englishman had reached the quayside where the French troops were already beginning to land. He was not afraid, telling himself that any disagreement was between the French and the Welsh and had nothing to do with him. However, he had been enjoying his holiday and was cross that it should be spoiled in this way. He approached a French officer who was directing the troops towards the town, and spoke to him in his own tongue.

'I do not know what you are doing in this town,' he said. 'No war has been declared and I can assure you that you cannot win any battle here. Wales is a country of brave fighting men and these of Pembrokeshire are no exception.'

'We do not come as an enemy of Wales,' replied the Frenchman. 'We are here to relieve our oppressed brothers.'

'Nonsense!' snapped the Englishman. 'No one is oppressed here. The Welsh have no argument with the English in this day and age, whatever may have happened in the past.'

During this conversation, one of the French soldiers removed the silver buckles from the Englishman's shoes while two others pilfered his knee buckles. Going further into the French lines, the gentleman was approached by another French officer who accused him of being improperly dressed.

'Certainly that is so,' came the haughty reply, 'and that I am without buckles to my shoes and to my knee breeches is the fault of your rough soldiery.' He pointed to a soldier whom he recognised as being one of the thieves. 'There is one of the culprits. Do something about it.'

Somewhat taken back, the French officer sentenced the man to immediate execution but this caused such a furore among the other soldiers who declared that nothing would induce them to shoot their comrade that the officer was forced to let the thief go.

'There is not much discipline here,' said the Englishman, 'where an officer's order can so easily be disobeyed.'

The Frenchman flushed and turned away, letting the Englishman return safely to the Fishguard hotel where he was staying.

By now, the local inhabitants had become aware that the French troops had arrived in their quiet country town. At first it had been thought that the approaching vessels were merchant ships seeking safety from an approaching gale but it was not long before anxiety was changed into alarm as boats were seen of armed men putting off from the ships. By midnight the boats ceased coming; all the soldiers has disembarked. However, it was so dark that it was impossible to ascertain the number of the force. Knots of local men filled the streets to discuss the invasion and it was decided to evacuate the women and children.

Next day the men of Fishguard armed themselves with pitchforks, scythes, pistols or whatever weapons they could snatch, determined to face the foe until the militia, warned by the farmer, could arrive. The French meanwhile, hungry and tired and deserted now by the ships in which they had arrived, were busy foraging. They laid their hands upon everything eatable in the neighbourhood. A few days before, a wreck with a cargo of spirits had occurred on the coast and every cottage was supplied with a cask. Soon the French soldiers were both drunk and overfed. Such discipline as there had been was now at an end.

The local men informed the enemy that if a shot were fired, they would close in on them at once. Soon a small troop of soldiers arrived from Haverfordwest and a parley with the French took place.

'How many have you?' demanded one of the French officers.

'Two thousand cavalry and the same number of well-trained infantry,' the Welsh officer lied bravely.

The Frenchman had his doubts about the truth of this but happened to look at that moment towards the hills behind the town where the women and children had been sent. A multitude of women stood there, row upon row of them, wearing the red flannel shawls and tall beaver hats as was their custom. They had the appearance to a foreign eye of a red coated regiment of soldiers.

'By God!' exclaimed the French officer. 'Truly you do not lie. We are outnumbered. Gives us twelve hours to capitulate.'

'I'll give you as many minutes,' snapped the English officer.

At two o'clock the enemy laid down their arms. That night they were marched away as prisoners. The feeling between the French officers and their men was so bad that the officers begged to be separated from them. The officers, therefore, were sent to Carmarthen and the privates were brought to Haverfordwest. Their numbers exceeded fourteen hundred. Many of the soldiers appeared to have the marks of fetters upon their legs and it was later assumed that they were criminals of whom the French government wished to be rid. Their behaviour certainly did not bear the mark of professional soldiers.

The whole happening had been almost farcial but thus ended the last French invasion of British soil.

Vortigern and the Dragons

Long, long ago in the sixth century, there lived a great man called Vortigern, the powerful ruler of part of Britain. But he betrayed his people when he paid the false Saxons to fight for him as mercenaries. Soon these mercenaries were joined by more men like them and Vortigern's power came to an end as the whole of southern Britain was ravaged by the Saxon hordes. Vortigern fled to Wales and set about building a fortress near Dinas Emrys in Caernarfonshire. There a high rock towered from the centre of a vale, overlooking the waters of Llyn Dinas and this was the spot Vortigern chose.

He began building his stronghold, but something strange began to happen. Each day a wall was built and, by the next evening, the wall had fallen down. This happened over and over again, puzzling and plagueing Vortigern until he was finally forced to send for a local magician.

'How can it be that every stone that is laid has fallen to the ground by the following morning?' he asked.

The magician pulled at his beard, frowned and went into a reverie. He spent a long time thinking over the problem and finally he spoke.

'This is not altogether a new problem. I have known it happen in other places. There is only one way that you may construct your castle without hindrance.'

'Speak on,' urged Vortigern. 'The sooner this matter is settled, the better.'

'It is not an easy answer I can give you. It involves a certain amount of patience.'

'Go on, go on,' cried Vortigern impatiently.

'Patience, I said patience,' chided the wizard. 'You must first find a boy who was born without a father. This boy must then be sacrificed on this mountain crag and his blood sprinkled on the stones.'

'Where do I look for such a boy?' asked Vortigern.

'Look to the south,' advised the magician, and would say no more.

The boy was finally found by Vortigern's men in a small village in South Wales; his name was Emrys and he was most unwilling to travel north, suspecting what his fate would be.

'I should prefer to stay here with my mother,' said Emrys. 'She has no-one else to look after her.'

The men merely growled at him, seized him and carried him northwards. When Vortigern set eyes on the boy, who was a handsome lad and carried himself well, he was almost sorry that such a boy had to be sacrificed.

'Why am I here?' asked Emrys. 'To my knowledge I have never done you any harm.'

'I need to sprinkle your blood on the foundation stones of the castle I am building,' replied Vortigern slowly. 'There is no other way to get it built. Each day the walls are partly finished and the next day they are down. No-one can explain it and only the wizard has an answer; that is why you are here.'

'There is another answer,' said Emrys, who was not without his own brand of magic.

'How can a mere boy know such a thing?'

'There is another answer,' replied Emrys, 'Please hear me out, my lord.'

Vortigern nodded; he liked the boy and was not averse to postponing his death.

'Below the foundations of your castle there is a lake and, at the bottom of the lake, there are two dragons fighting. One dragon is white and represents the Saxons; the other is red and represents Wales. Their terrible battle has gone on for a long time and it is this that shakes down the walls of your castle every night.'

Vortigern was astounded. 'How may I believe you?' he asked.

'Did your magician give you a better explanation?' asked the boy.

'He gave me no explanation, only a cure.'

'Listen to me then; order a well to be sunk,' said Emrys, 'and find out the truth of what I say.'

Vortigern gave the order and, sure enough, the lake was found, deep below the foundation of the castle. A great roar was heard and the air became hot and steamy as the two huge

Vortigern and the Dragons

dragons rose towards the sky, their claws flailing and their teeth sunk into each other's horny flesh.

A fierce battle followed in the air, sometimes the red dragon seemed to be winning and the next moment the white one fought back and appeared to be the stronger. For hours the battle raged as Vortigern and his followers looked on in amazement. Only Emrys appeared to be unimpressed. It was, after all, only what he had expected. Finally, making an enormous effort, the red dragon overpowered the white one which fell to the ground, never to rise again. The red dragon flew off, bellowing forth flames and smoke and swishing his long tail to and fro with an air of triumph.

'Wales has won!' exclaimed Emrys, 'surely now Wales will certainly survive.'

So Vortigern built his castle without any further disasters and Emrys returned to his village in South Wales, happy that he had so narrowly escaped with his life.

Alice

It was towards the end of the 19th century when Alice and her sisters Lorina and Edith Liddell sat in the sitting room of a house called Pen Morfa in Llandudno where they and their parents stayed each summer. On this particular day it was raining hard and the three little girls were chatting away to each other in order to pass the time. Edith and Lorina were lively little girls and were playing happily with their dolls whilst Alice with her long straight hair was talking to them now and then but mainly gazed out of the window, dreaming dreams, and longing for the rain to stop so that she might wander over the sand dunes on the West shore where she could hitch up her cumbersome clothes and paddle in the warm clear sea.

'We are having a visitor tonight,' announced Edith suddenly.

'Who's coming?' asked Lorina. 'One of Papa's boring friends?'

Mr. Liddell was Dean of Christchurch, Oxford, a serious man who had once written a history of Ancient Rome which none of his three daughters found at all interesting.

'It's that quiet man who blushes and stammers,' Edith replied. 'You know who I mean, that mathematics man. I heard Mama mention it this morning.'

'Not Mr. Dodgson!' exlaimed Alice. 'Why he's quite my favourite of Papa's friends. How long is he staying?'

'About a week, I think,' said Edith. 'But I don't know what you see in him, he's so shy.'

'He tells the most wonderful stories,' said Alice. 'I could listen to him all day long.'

'Men who know only about arithmetic and Algebra and all that cannot possibly tell stories that would appeal to us.'

'You're wrong,' replied Alice quietly, 'quite, quite wrong.'

Mr. Dodgson arrived that evening just in time to see the three girls before they went to bed. His conversation with Dean Liddell and his wife had been very one-sided as the visitor seemed unable to say much to them. They were a very kind couple and tried hard to make him feel at home, but he had scarcely uttered one word and sat now quietly smoking his pipe in a corner of the room where he could not easily be seen but, when the children appeared in their pretty lace trimmed nightgowns, he moved forward to see them better and his eyes lit up when he saw what appeared to be three little angels, although their father disillusioned Mr. Dodgson, saying they were more like little devils most of the time. But he smiled as he said it and no-one took offence. The children lined up to kiss their parents goodnight and almost immediately Mr. Dodgson began to talk to them and stammered but a little as he spoke. It was Alice who talked back. Lorina and Edith were not so impressed with this stange young man even though he did produce some delicious chocolates from inside the pocket where he normally kept his pipe.

'Do you remember, Alice, that lovely day when we were together on the river at Oxford?' asked Mr. Dodgson.

Alice remembered it well for it had been a most marvellous day when he had told her some marvellous stories.

As Mr. Dodgson went on chatting easily with the children, he now produced from the same large pocket some puzzles and a few small toys. He knew exactly the games and toys the children most enjoyed and they went to bed, happy with their new gifts.

'There you see,' said Alice once she was in bed, 'I told you Mr. Dodgson is a very nice, kind man.'

Her two sisters nodded their small, sleepy heads and admitted that Alice was right. Even so, the next day Edith and Lorina preferred to go for a drive in the pony and trap with their mother and father while Alice said she would prefer to go for a walk with Mr. Dodgson. They made their way towards the sand hills and rabbit warrens where they sat down and munched some sweets which the young man produced from the same pocket which had revealed such a wonderful supply of interesting things the night before.

'Mr. Dodgson,' said Alice as soon as they had settled down, 'will you please tell me a story with plenty of nonsense in it?'

Mr. Dodgson smiled his shy smile. 'All my stories have plenty of nonsense in them. Look over there, Alice, can you see that little rabbit scuttling away over the sand dunes?'

Alice followed his pointing finger and nodded her head.

'Then let's have a story about a rabbit. How about that?'

'Oh yes, please please and could I be in the story with the rabbit?'

'That is possible,' said Mr. Dodgson, trying to look very serious. 'Here begins the story of Alice and the white rabbit. "Alice was beginning to get very tired . . ." '

'But I'm not at all tired,' protested Alice.

'For the purpose of this story,' said her friend, 'you are very tired so please do not interrupt me again.' He sounded cross but, at the same time, he winked at Alice and pulled a funny face which made her laugh.

'But that wasn't a white rabbit we saw,' interupted Alice again. 'It was an ordinary brown rabbit.'

'There will be nothing ordinary about my rabbit,' Mr. Dodgson assured her. And he began to tell the little girl a most extraordinary story. He was nowhere near the end of it when he looked at his watch and said it was high time they went home for luncheon.

Edith and Lorina were so busy telling Alice what they had seen on their ride that they were not as interested as Alice would like them to have been when she told them about Mr. Dodgson's story.

'It is the most wonderful story and he is going to continue it tomorrow,' said Alice, 'and then you can hear it, too.'

But when the next morning came, although all three little girls went for a walk with their visitor, Lorina and Edith went to look for shells on the beach while Alice settled down to listen to more of Mr. Dodgson's remarkable story, a bubbling delight of strange characters who did very strange things. Each day Alice listened, entranced, as the tale continued until finally, and before it was finished, the Liddell's guest departed and returned to Oxford where he lived.

Now there was something special about those walks with Mr. Dodgson, something special about Alice Liddell and something very special about the story. Alice was made the heroine of the fictional 'Alice in Wonderland', a book that is perhaps the most famous of all children's books and it was written by a man called Lewis Carroll, whose real name was Dodgson, and the inspiration had come to him during his stay in Llandudno.

Many, years later, in 1933, a famous Welsh politician unveiled a memorial to Lewis Carroll, a statue of the White Rabbit and some of the immortal characters who lived in this magical of books. So many children have paid a visit to this statue to shake the paw of the White Rabbit that it actually fell off a few years later.

Let us leave the last word to Mr. Lloyd George who said, 'Lewis Carroll radiates happiness and the world today is a happier place because he passed through it. It is great thing for you in Llandudno to know that he drew inspiration from your sea and your mountains and that it was the hand of a little child who led him.'

Prince Madoc

Most people if asked who discovered America would reply 'Christopher Columbus, of course' but there are some Welshmen who would not agree with this, saying that Prince Madoc, son of Owain Gwyneth who owned land in North Wales, discovered America at least two centuries before Columbus. Now follows the kind of story that might have happened.

Thomas, son of a lord who served Madoc, was nearly fourteen when his father sent for him to discuss his future.

'You know that Madoc takes a great interest in you, my boy,' said Thomas's father, 'and I have a suggestion to make with which you may agree or disagree, as you please. You know I have never forced you to anything you did not want to do.'

Thomas was puzzled; his father appeared both serious and a little troubled.

'I'll do anything you ask of me, father,' he said.

'Perhaps, son, it would be better if you talked to Prince Madoc himself and not to me,' suggested his father.

So Thomas went to see the prince who had a high regard for Thomas's father.

'Father said I should talk to you about something, sire, which apparently he does not wish to discuss with me.'

Madoc smiled. 'Well, boy, you are nearly a man now and, as you know, I am as happy at sea as on land, unlike most Welshmen who have no reputation for being good sailors. I am taking two ships to explore a far land across the Atlantic Ocean.'

'Across the Ocean!' exclaimed Thomas, 'but surely, if you sail to the west, our ships will go over the edge of the world and that would be the end of them.'

Madoc laughed. 'That is a foolish attitude to take. The world I believe to be round. It is only landlubbers who think otherwise.'

'But what is all this to do with me anyway?' asked Thomas.

'I'll come straight to the point, I should like you to be part of my crew. I have spoken to your father about this and he has reluctantly agreed that you should come with me, but only if you wish to do so.'

Thomas was so astounded by these words that for a moment he could think of nothing to say.

'Come, come, boy, make up your mind quickly. I have little time for trivial conversation nor for your silence. Just let me say I should like your answer.'

'But why me?' asked Thomas.

'Because of the regard I have for your father who has always been a man of courage and intelligence and I hope some of this will have rubbed off on you.'

'But why not ask my father to go with you then, instead of me?'

'He is too old, and anyway I do not necessarily need an experienced sailor. I want a boy like you to help the cook, to scrub the decks and to wait on me. I'll have you on my ship, not on the other ship accompanying me, but where I can keep a friendly eye on you. Now what do you think?'

'I should love it,' said Thomas instantly. 'It will be the most exciting thing I have ever done and I am truly grateful that you ask me to go with you. I go with you wherever you may sail, and if there is land beyond the Atlantic Ocean, who knows what treasure we may find.'

'It is land, not treasure I am looking for, my lad. There is so much to be learned about the new world and to be the first westerner to find such a place would mean as much to me as a thousand pieces of gold.'

A few weeks went by until the ships of Madoc were ready to sail, weeks during which Thomas became more and more excited at the thought of the adventure which lay ahead of him. However, when the day arrived to set sail from Aber-Cerrig-Gwynion near Rhos-on-Sea, Thomas began to have butterflies in his stomach. The ships were primitive compared to our modern standards, being made of wood with sails of canvas and some with oars to help them on their way. The ship Prince Madoc commanded and on which Thomas worked was called Gwenna Garn or, in English Horn Gwenna.

In 1170, the day on which they sailed was balmy and the sea calm and blue. Thomas was sure he was going to enjoy the long journey ahead but, alas, when they had been out at sea for only a couple of days, the weather changed. The wind arose and the sea became turbulent with great waves sweeping over the deck of the ship. Thomas began to feel very ill but still tried to carry out his duties. He was sickened by the sight of the food he had to prepare for Madoc and his officers. He could scarcely stand on his feet to sweep the deck and, at night, the swinging of the hammock in which he slept was such that he was often unable to get any sleep at all.

Many months went by and poor Thomas felt no better. At last Madoc cried out in triumph.

'Look, look, there is land just ahead; look, you must look!'

Captain and crew were elated but Thomas was beyond caring except that the thought of his feet on dry land instead of the nightmare he had been enduring was something to be welcomed. The two ships docked in a place that was later to be named Mobile Bay, in Alabama. As soon as Thomas was able to leave the ship, he shouted with joy when he left the vessel which had hardly been very kind to him, or so he thought.

Many more months went by as Madoc and his crew settled in the lush countryside where fish were easily caught and birds and deer killed by the archer's bow. One day, a few strange people arrived silently in what was now Madoc's settlement. They looked savage, with their faces painted bright colours, but their approach was gentle. They were members of a race which was later mistakenly called Red Indian and this particular tribe was known as the Mandans. Thomas was astonished to learn that such a primitive people should know as much as these Mandans knew. They could follow trails, were efficient with the bow and arrow, treated their wives well and lived in tents that were better than many of the hovels Thomas had seen at home in Wales.

Thomas had just begun to enjoy himself, learning some words of the Mandan language and, in return teaching them some words of Welsh, when Madoc announced that it was time to leave and make for home, to tell his wonderful story of the new country he had found to his fellow Welshmen. There were calm days and stormy days when it seemed the ship might sink and the story never told. Thomas felt better on the return journey than he had felt when they had first set out on the adventure. The journey that today would take only a matter of hours took, in the year 1170, over a year, and when the ships arrived back at what is now call Port Madoc, there was great excitement among local lords and the ordinary country folk, all of whom had been convinced they would never again see Madoc and his sailors. All Thomas was able to say to his father was, 'I had never known such a wonderful place as America could ever have existed. We saw only a tiny bit of it but there must be miles and miles of it still undiscovered. I would not have missed such an experience and shall remember it to my dying day.'

But his attitude changed when, some time later, Madoc sent for him again.

'Now young Thomas, you are more of a man than the boy I first took on our voyage of discovery, are you not? Well, I am sailing again. Are you coming with me?'

Thomas was silent and Madoc repeated his question. This time Thomas blushed and Madoc let out a cry of surprise.

'Do you not wish to see again what we witnessed last time?'

'It's not that, sire, not that,' mumbled Thomas.

Madoc grinned. 'You need go no further; I know what troubles you. You liked the destination but hated the journey. Am I right?'

Thomas hung his head and agreed that this was so. He could never forget those months of hardship. It was with some regret, however, that he saw Madoc set sail without him.

Madoc was never seen again in Wales but it is possible that he safely reached the shores of Alabama once more, and that he and his men mixed with the Indian Mandan tribe. For example, it is certain that the Mandan tribe, which died out in the last century, possessed words in the language which appeared to be Welsh and, unlike other Red Indians, there were some of them bearded and blue-eyed. Whether we believe the story of Madoc and his ships or are sceptical of the whole story, it is interesting to note that, as recently as 1953, a Ladies' Society called 'Daughters of Revolution' actually erected a memorial tablet at Fort Morgan, Mobile Bay, Alabama, bearing these words:

'In memory of Prince Madoc, a Welsh explorer, who landed on the shores of Mobile Bay, Alabama, in 1170 and left behind, with the Indians, the Welsh language.'

The Buccaneer

Unlike Madoc, Henry Morgan was a landsman rather than a seaman, even though he is thought of as one of the great pirates of his age. He was born at Tredegar in South Wales, the son of a landowner, in the year 1655. He was of average height but burly and pictures of him show him to have had a typical Welsh bullet head. He was handsome in a bold way, good eyes, straight nose and full-lipped mouth. As was the fashion, he wore a flowing wig and had a moustache and small beard.

As a young man, he had a sense of adventure which took him from a luxurious home to Cardiff and from there to Bristol where he heard lurid tales of some of the men of the Caribbean and the gold and jewels which they plundered. He joined a ship, brimming with a sense of spirit and ambition. He had a hard time on board but worse was to come. The ship foundered and Henry was captured, taken to Barbados and sold as a bondsman.

Morgan was a born leader and escaped from bondage with a band of other slaves as ruthless as he was himself. The image of a pirate is often of someone romantic and brave. Morgan certainly had enormous courage but gathered around him an army of ruffians who, like him, would stop at nothing. They fought; they plundered; they looted. French and Spanish ships alike were good targets for rich picking. The profits were huge and, at the height of his success, Morgan was ordered to return to England to face charges of bad behaviour. There he met and so charmed King Charles that he was made governor of Jamaica and was knighted into the bargain. No doubt some of his profits went into the royal coffers in return for these favours. Henry had risen to great heights.

He was too restless a spirit to stay quietly in Jamaica. His sights were now set on the wealth that could be found in Panama where he had his eyes on the capture of a Spanish galleon sailing with a cargo of treasure and a few passengers. The figure of the treasure was said to amount to millions of pieces of eight. This particular galleon was never, in fact, conquered although

Morgan had commissioned four of the best ships for the expedition. Henry blamed the men in charge for their failure owing to their gluttony and drunkenness, several rich wines having been found on the ship. In desperation, the band of rogues found a smaller merchant vessel just arrived in Tobago whose cargo was fairly valuable. The buccaneers also raided Tobaga Island, taking prisoners a number of refugees and many slaves.

Sir Henry Morgan was a cruel man who behaved appallingly to his military enemies and the civilians whom he captured. However, there is one tale about him which shows he had a modicum of gallant chivalry, and this occurred soon after the capture of that particular Spanish galleon. Most women prisoners usually had a very hard time from Morgan and his army. But more noble women were given better treatment in the hope that a ransom might be raised for their release.

Among the women captured at Tobago was the wife of a merchant, going to join her husband in Peru. She is not named in history but we shall call her Maria. Maria was a lady of quality, virtuous, young and extremely beautiful. When Morgan first saw her, his usual hard character warmed and softened. He had her brought to the patio of his residence, a place of tiled walks, flowering shrubs and plants about a fountain with parrots swinging on hoops and tortoises near a pool. Sunlight streamed between the leaves and Sir Henry Morgan hoped that these lovely surroundings would have a good effect on Maria. He said little to her but gazed at her amorously and hoped the garden would impress her. She said even less and appeared to take no notice of her surroundings. She held herself erectly and faced her captor with fearless eyes.

'I will give you anything you desire,' said Henry at last.

'My freedom,' replied Maria coldly.

'That, madam, alas is the one thing I cannot grant.'

'Then there is no more to be said between us,' came the disdainful reply.

'Oh yes, there is indeed, I wish you to have a room in my palace and a negro woman to look after your every need.'

'It would suit me better to be left with the other prisoners,' retorted Maria.

Morgan smiled at her. She was a real beauty, this one, and with spirit, too. Maria did not smile back.

Morgan ignored her request and, true to his word, placed Maria in one of the best rooms in his palatial house with not only a negro woman to look after her but many other servants, too. She had every comfort and the best food and wines the house could supply. Every day Morgan visited her, paying her lavish compliments and anxious to please her in every way. She never replied to anything he said except when, on one occasion, she asked him to leave her alone as she was at her prayers. Morgan left without a murmur.

One day, he came back to her with a very special question.

'Madam,' he said, 'I have gazed upon your beauty and admired your virtue. To be honest, I wish to marry you.'

Maria was aghast. 'Sir Henry Morgan,' she replied coldly and with dignity, 'may I remind you I am already married.'

'Oh we can forget about that merchant in Peru; he is of no importance. We can be happy together without thinking of him.'

'And do we also forget a certain Mary Elizabeth in Jamaica to whom, I understand, you are already married?'

Morgan flushed for it was true what she had said. 'Yes,' he replied boldly, 'we may forget about her, too.'

After a few days had elapsed and still Maria would scarcely speak to him, Morgan lost patience. Indeed Maria had said she would rather kill herself than marry him. So the Governor of Jamaica cast the poor lady into a dark and stinking prison with only rats for company and allowed her the minimum of food and water. Maybe he hoped she would now give in to his proposal but her gaolers reported that the lady spent her days in prayer and never asked to see Sir Henry. Then, having failed to make Maria change her mind, he dispatched her to join her sisters in some more comfortable accommodation and named the price of her ransom to a higher figure.

Maria assured her friends that she thought no harm would come to them as long as the ransoms asked were paid. Maria had been brought up to believe like every other Spanish lady that buccaneers were heretical and scarcely human.

'But,' she said, 'I have heard this Sir Henry Morgan curse in the name of God so I believe he must be a Christian.'

Finally, she was allowed, like the other high-born women, to send messengers into the interior to find her husband.

'I am sending two of my men to collect ransom for your freedom,' said Sir Henry when next he demanded to see her.

Alas for Maria, the next time she saw him, Morgan had to say, 'I regret, madam, that my men have stolen the money your husband sent for you. They will, of course, be severely punished for this.'

For the first time Maria broke down and wept. Morgan's heart was softened at the sight of her tears.

'Why do you weep? I have already offered you my protection,' he said.

'I cannot hope to raise another ransom,' she replied. 'My husband had sent as much as he could afford. There can be no more money forthcoming.'

'Do you suppose I will make you suffer for the rascality of two thieves,' said Morgan softly, realising at last that Maria had no intention of marrying him.

He had a horse brought to her and wished her well for the journey.

'You are free as you have always wished to be,' he said.

She smiled at him for the first and last time. She was small and slim, an olive skinned beauty with glossy black hair. She rode the horse with the grace of a Spanish woman in the saddle. The hoofs of her horse clattered on the pebbles, the silver bells on its trappings jingled as she went. Morgan watched her go; he actually wiped tears from his eyes. He lifted his hand in farewell to the woman he loved. Maria did not even turn her head to acknowledge what was probably the most generous act in his life of this famous Welshman, cruel but brave Sir Henry Morgan.